EVACUEES

Andy Kempe and Rick Holroyd

imaging

EVACUEES

Andy Kempe and Rick Holroyd

Hodder & Stoughton

LONDON SYDNEY AUCKLAND

ACKNOWLEDGEMENTS

The publishers would like to thank the following for giving permission to use copyright photographs in this book.

p11, Hulton-Deutsch Collection; p12tl, Institute of Agriculture History and Museum of Rural Life, University of Reading, Berkshire; p12tr, Imperial War Museum; p12b, Watford Central Library; p15, Popperfoto; p16, Topham Picture Source; p21, Hulton-Deutsch Collection; p25, Imperial War Museum; p28, Popperfoto; p29, Hulton-Deutsch Collection; p33, 36, 38, Topham Picture Source; p47, Imperial War Museum; p50, Hulton-Deutsch Collection; p52tl, Hulton-Deutsch Collection; p52bl, br, Topham Picture Source; p56t, Topham Picture Source; P56b, 57t, b, Watford Museum; p60, Cadbury's; p63, Theale C.E. Primary School, Berkshire; p67t, Popperfoto; p67b, Panos Pictures; p68, Topham Picture Source.

Every effort has been made to trace and acknowledge ownership of copyright. The publishers will be glad to make suitable arrangements with any copyright holders whom it has not been possible to contact.

British Library Cataloguing in Publication Data

Kempe, Andy
  Imaging: evacuees. — (Imaging)
  I. Title   II. Holroyd, Rick   III. Series
  792.1

ISBN 0 340 54836 3

First published 1993

Typeset by MULTIPLEX Techniques Ltd, St Mary Cray, Kent.
Printed in Great Britain for the educational publishing division of Hodder & Stoughton Ltd, Mill Road, Dunton Green, Sevenoaks, Kent by Thomson Litho Ltd, East Kilbride.

CONTENTS

INTRODUCTION

evacuate   to throw out the contents of; to discharge; to remove, as
             from a place of danger; to clear out troops, inhabitants
             from.
evacuee   a person removed in an evacuation.

How much do you know about World War Two?
The truth is, you probably know a great deal just from films and stories
you have come across. Even if you don't know anyone who was directly
involved in the fighting, you probably know someone who remembers it
happening. These people may have astonishing tales to tell you about
what it was like.

   In this book, you will read the stories of four people who were
involved in one particular event of the war – EVACUATION. There are
many other stories you can discover for yourselves, from people you
know. Some will be funny, some sad and some incredible, but – best of
all – they will all be true. Some stories, like the fourth one in the book,
have never become well known. The question is, why not?

TASKS

1   What words come into your head when
you think about World War Two? Try to fill
a sheet of paper or the blackboard with
words and ideas about:

– who was involved;   – when it happened;
– what happened;   – what it was like.

(Don't worry about being right or wrong.
The point is just to put down what you *think*
it was all about.)

2   In small groups, discuss the words and
ideas that you have collected. Do any of you
know any more about the War? Perhaps you
know someone who was involved? Maybe
you've seen some films about it? Write down

three things to do with the War that you
would like to find out about.

3   In your groups, check your own ideas
about the War against the list of the main
events on p. 5. Discuss any words or details
that you don't understand.

4   Using any of the ideas that you have
talked about so far, make up a short scene to
show what you think life was like for people
of your own age during the War.

   Show your scene to the rest of the class.
Do they agree with your ideas? Watch other
groups' scenes. Are they believable, or are
they 'action-packed', like a lot of war films?

MAIN EVENTS

1939 March   Hitler's army invades Czechoslovakia.
      Aug.   Hitler threatens to invade Poland.
              Britain promises to protect Poland.
      Sept.   German troops march into Poland. The evacuation plan is put into action.
      Sept.   Britain declares war on Germany.
              By the end of September, almost one third of all Britons have been evacuated.
      Dec.   Many evacuees return home for Christmas. There has been no bombing so many stay at home.

1940 Jan.   Rationing of food starts.
      May   Hitler invades Belgium, Luxembourg and Holland.
      June   British troops are evacuated from Dunkirk.
              The Germans take over France.
      Aug.   The Battle of Britain starts. German aircraft attack RAF stations in an attempt to destroy the airforce.
      Sept.   Start of the 'Blitz'. Three million homes are destroyed, 30,000 people are killed.
      Nov.   Nightly bombing of London finishes.

1941 June   Clothes are rationed.
              Germany invades Russia.
      Dec.   Japan bombs the American fleet (Pearl Harbour).
              America declares war on Japan and Germany.

1942   American army arrives in Britain.
              Food and clothing in very short supply.

1943 March – Heavy bombing of German towns.
      Sept.

1944 June   D-Day. British and American forces invade France.
              Germans launch flying bombs (V-1s) against Britain. A new evacuation starts from London.
      Dec.   V-2 bombs dropped on London.

1945 May   Russian army reaches Berlin.
              Germany surrenders.
      Aug.   Americans drop first atomic bombs on Japan. Hiroshima and Nagasaki completely destroyed.
              Japan surrenders. The War is over.

KIM:

What was it like to be evacuated?

When the children were evacuated, what did they think would happen to them?

Read the story below before moving on to explore the questions.

Let me try to put things in order. I haven't exactly had the chance before. Besides, there's nothing else to do. I thought this was going to be dead exciting this journey. It's not. It's dead boring. Well, this bit is anyway. We've been stuck in this railway siding for nearly an hour. What if a Jerry came and bombed us? We're a sitting target stuck here. Mind, if everyone else on this train is like me, they wouldn't know what a German plane looked like.

All right. Tell it in order. What's happened.

I suppose it was a relief in the end when war was declared. Everyone had been going on about it happening for ages before it actually did. At least now we know where we stand. Every night for weeks Dad had sat down in his chair after tea, turned on the wireless, rolled a cigarette and said, 'Well, let's hear the worst'.

Well, now we know the worst. Now everybody knows. Now we're all to be sent away. 'Evacuated' they call it. We're the 'evacuees'. Sent away from home in case 'they' come.

If they come, which I doubt. I looked on the map in the Geography room in school to see where Germany was. It's miles away. Even if they did try it, all their bombers would be shot down before they got up here.

They sent loads of kids away from London before the Prime Minister even said we were at war. But I didn't think we'd have to go. Even when Mum packed the suitcase I thought it was just her being daft as usual. George Atkinson's Mum sent him away months back. When nothing happened he came home again. We'd creep up on him and shout, 'Watch it, George, there's a bomb!' Then we'd laugh. Doesn't seem very funny now.

The worst thing about 'the War' so far for me is that I have to lug this ruddy gas mask around with me every day. The corners of the box scratch against the side of your legs as you go along and make them sore. We got them weeks back just in case the

Germans made a surprise attack. Every day we practise putting them on quickly. I don't know how many times I've been asked 'Have you got your gas mask? Let's see it.' When we first got them they were good fun. Mind, you had to be careful not to get caught playing with them. They're dead good for blowing raspberries in. I think they're just a flipping nuisance now. They stink of rubber and you can't hardly breathe. Also, the little perspex panel gets all misty and you can't see out. Dad says that in the First War the Germans used gas bombs and if you breathed in the gas it would turn your lungs into tomato soup. I don't really know what he meant by that. The little kids have masks with ears on like Mickey Mouse. I've seen the teachers play a game to get the little 'uns to put them on quickly. They make it into a competition.

But in order. Let's tell it in order.

Well, there was the letter. I came home from school and Mum was sitting quietly by the fire reading it. When I came in she smiled, but I could see she'd been crying. She told me to go up and wash my hands ready for tea and I noticed my case, all packed up, at the foot of the stairs.

We had tea and she didn't mention the letter, but when Dad came home he read it to me. I didn't hardly understand it when I saw it, so it was a good job Dad explained it. It was a bit of a shock when the penny dropped. Even though it had been talked about so much, I still couldn't really believe it. Mum and Dad talked most of last night. I couldn't hear what they were saying, but I think Mum was crying again. When I got up, Dad had already gone to work. Mum said he'd kissed me goodbye and left a letter for me. I haven't opened it yet. Mum walked to school with me just like she had on the first day. It was a lovely morning. On the way we passed a whole load of kids from the boarding school getting onto a bus with PRIVATE on the front. When we got to school the playground was already full. Our lot looked very different from the boarding school kids. The teachers came and checked our labels and gas masks. Everyone's got a label saying who they are and what their address is. Look like a load of parcels, we do. We had to stand and wait ages 'til everybody that should have been there was there. I kissed Mum goodbye, then we marched off to the station. Lots of the Mums were crying, some of the little'uns too. I'm glad mine didn't start.

I've only ever been on a train twice before, and then not very far. Some of the others have never been on one. Where my Uncle

Bill and Aunty Vera live you can see the countryside and even walk across some fields. I tried to describe it to some of the others while we were waiting at Midland Station but it's hard. Funny to think of people actually living in the country.

It wasn't 'til I saw Midland Station moving away that I realised I hadn't a clue where we were going. We went a little way, then the train stopped and started going backwards. Everybody cheered. I think we probably thought the War had been called off and we were going home again. We weren't though. We were just getting onto a different line. It's getting dark now. Can't really see where we are. Ah! We're moving again.

No-one's cheering though.

QUESTIONS *to think and talk about*

- Where is Kim during this passage? Why is she there?
- What is her attitude towards the War, and towards leaving home?
- Is there anything about Kim's story that you find particularly surprising or interesting?

As people like Kim sat on these trains in 1939 they didn't know:

- where they were going;
- how long the War would last;
- what hardships they would suffer;
- what dreadful new weapons would be used.

And perhaps worst of all:

- what they would find when they eventually came home.

- How do you think you would feel if you were in Kim's situation?

TASKS

1 From the questions above, you already know quite a lot about Kim. Make up some more details about her that you think fit. For example, how old is she? Where does she live? What sort of school does she go to? Make up at least three more details about her.

If you could ask Kim one question about herself or her situation, what would you ask?

2 In small groups, use Kim's story and any of your own details about her to devise a scene. Try to show what sort of character she is. You know how she feels about being evacuated, but what does she think about other things? What does she like or dislike? What is she good or bad at doing?

SOME BACKGROUND

The map below shows what Europe looked like in 1939. If you compare it with a modern map, you will see that the size and shape of countries such as Germany, Poland and Czechoslovakia has changed. For Kim, as for many people, the trouble brewing between those countries seemed a long way off, and not likely to have much effect on life in Britain. Just a few days before war broke out, four out of five people did not think it would actually happen.

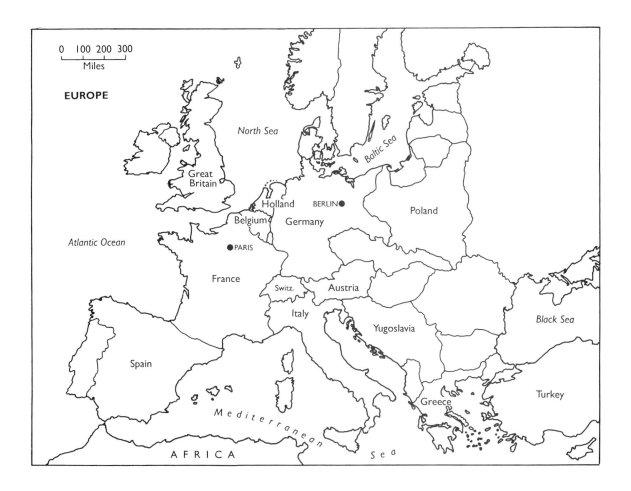

One hundred years ago, the idea of British towns and cities being bombed from the air would have seemed ridiculous. For a start, there were no aeroplanes!

London was bombed in the First World War by balloons called Zeppelins. Over 1000 Londoners were killed by bombs during that war.

By 1939, aeroplanes had become fast and powerful. Some people realised that cities in every part of the country could be reached by enemy aircraft. But to other people, like Kim, the idea of an aeroplane coming all the way from Germany to drop bombs still seemed impossible.

Plans were made to take people out of the cities to safety in the country. Not everyone could go – men and women were needed to work in the city factories.

By 1 September, 1939, war seemed certain. The evacuation plan was put into action. These were the people who were evacuated:

– 827,000 unaccompanied children;
– 524,000 mothers with their children aged under five;
– 13,000 pregnant women;
– 7000 blind, crippled and handicapped people;
– 113,000 school teachers or escorts for children.

The map below shows the towns from which people were evacuated. Which is the closest one to you? Who might be able to tell you where people from that town were sent?

TASKS

1   How far away from your home town is Germany? How many of your class have been to Germany or know anything about what it is like there now? Changes are still happening in Europe. Try to find out about some of these, and why they are happening.

2   Work in small groups, and imagine that one or two of you have gone back in time to 1939. You meet Kim and her friends. What do you tell them about the War? Would they believe what you tell them? (Use the map of Europe on p. 9 and the chart of events on p. 5 to help you to explain what will happen.)

3   As a whole class, imagine that you are the people responsible for the national evacuation plan. It is August 1939 and it looks like there is going to be a war. Make a list of all the things you will have to decide. For example:

- which towns should be evacuated first;
- where the safest places would be to send the evacuees;
- how you will find homes for them;
- when you should evacuate;
- what instructions you should give to parents.

Set up an operations room. Divide the tasks up among smaller groups. When all the groups have decided how they intend to carry out their particular task, call a meeting and share your decisions.

GAS MASKS

Gas was used by both the British and German armies in the First World War. It was a terrifying weapon. Many people thought that gas bombs would also be dropped in the new war, and were anxious to protect their children from its effects.

Fortunately, no gas bombs were dropped by either side during the Second World War. However, everyone had to carry a gas mask with them at all times. There were special ones for babies, and even for dogs!

Hitler will send no warning –
so always carry your gas mask

ISSUED BY THE MINISTRY OF HOME SECURITY

What is your reaction to these photographs? What do you think it would be like to wear a gas mask?

You may know an elderly person who has kept his or her gas mask. Perhaps there is a local museum which has one. Either way, try to get hold of one. Smell it. Feel it. Put it on. Imagine having to wear one.

Here are some memories of gas masks:

We all had the standard black ones except my little sister. She had a red one with a red nose on it that flapped up and down. The one my baby brother had was issued with something like a cradle with a window on top. When Mum put him in it, he screamed and kicked up such a fuss; so Mum said, 'That's it! If we're going to die we'll all die together.' She then threw the gas masks away.

... the awful choking sensation and sweating inside that rubber mask which had to be ripped off like one's own skin.

We all hated putting on the gas masks at school and many were taken off full of tears.

TASKS

1 Imagine that you have been given a gas mask. Mime putting it on. What words can you think of that would describe the experience of wearing it? Try to use the words as the basis for a poem which describes somebody's first experience of a gas mask.

2 In small groups, imagine that you are Kim's classmates. You have been asked to invent a game which will help young children to get their masks on quickly without frightening them. Try out your games on each other and discuss how effective they would be with small children.

3 Design a poster which you think would have encouraged young people to look after their masks and keep them handy at all times. Any writing on the poster should be clear and easy to read.

4 How would a soldier who had been gassed in the First World War react to the issue of gas masks? What sort of memories might it bring back? Devise a scene which shows what happens when some children play with their gas masks in front of their grandfather.

THE CALL TO GO

This is a copy of a letter which was sent to all houses in one district in 1939. Read it carefully.

EVACUATION

In the event of an Emergency, arrangements have been made to evacuate school children from the London area to safe places in the country. It is hoped that your child/children will participate in this scheme. On receipt of further instructions, he/she/they should report to Star Road School bringing with him/her/them hat, raincoat, haversack containing night-clothes, towel, soap, toothbrush and toothpaste, and he/she/they should wear a card round his/her/their neck(s) giving his/her/their full names(s), age(s), school, home address and names of next of kin.

TASKS

1   How easy is this letter to understand? What do you think it is saying?

Work in small groups. Imagine that you are a family living in 1939. One afternoon you come home to find this letter on the doormat. Make a tableau (still image) which shows the family's reaction to the letter.

Compare your work with other groups. What different reactions are shown?

Make your own tableau again. When everyone is in position, count to three, then bring the image to life and play out the scene that follows.

2   If you were only allowed *one small suitcase or bag* to take away with you, what would you pack? Make a list, and remember that you have no idea how long you will be gone for.

Look carefully at the list you have made. Would most young people in 1939 have had all of those things?

Mime packing your case and speak aloud your feelings about this. Do any of the things you are packing have a special value to you?

Use your ideas from this to write a poem. The title might be, 'Things I'll Miss', or simply, 'Leaving'.

3   Choose one of the following scene outlines and develop it into an improvisation or written script.

(a) A family sit down and have tea together the evening before the children are due to be evacuated. In what way is this different from their usual teatime?

(*b*) In order to cheer themselves up, a group of evacuees tell each other why they think going away will be good fun.

(*c*) A group of children have gone to school one morning, certain of being evacuated that day. Late that afternoon, they return home with the news that the plans have been postponed. How is the news received?

(*d*) A family are told that the ship their children were on has been torpedoed on its voyage to Canada. Who tells them the news? How is it done?

Kim mentions that on the way to her school, she passes some children from the boarding school getting on to a bus marked PRIVATE. She also says that 'her lot' looked rather different.

Look at the picture below and compare it with the picture over the page.

QUESTIONS *to think and talk about*

- What differences can you see between the way the children are dressed?
- What sorts of luggage do they have?
- How would you describe the general atmosphere in each picture?
- How do you think the different groups will react to being sent away?

TASKS

1 In small groups, position yourselves like the children in *one* of the pictures shown. Play out the scene by saying what you think would be said in that situation.

After a few minutes, stop and talk about your work. Select about ten lines which fit the picture well. Write them down as a piece of script. Rehearse the scene and then present your work to the rest of the class. Compare the different attitudes and atmosphere each group has created.

2 In pairs, label yourselves A and B. A has seen a number of children being evacuated earlier in the day and is telling B about it. B wants to know as many details as possible about what was happening and what it was like. Act out their conversation. What questions does B ask? How easy is it for A to answer them?

3 Imagine that you are a newspaper reporter from 1939 who has been asked to write a story to go with these two pictures. What would you write?

THE JOURNEY

Being evacuated meant different things to different people. Some children had never been away from home before. Many city children had never seen the countryside or sea. For some, the whole thing must have been terrifying; others must have thought it a tremendous adventure.

Look at these memories from people who were evacuated:

We didn't cry because we didn't really know what was happening to us.

I thought it was an outing to the seaside. I looked out of the window and saw my mother crying. I said to my brother, 'What's Mummy crying for?'.

We were told that the order to evacuate might come through at any moment . . . So all that week we came to school in the morning, after fond farewells and the hurried making of sandwiches, and all that week we returned home in the evening and ate our sandwiches for supper . . . On Thursday the uncertainty was ended . . . We marched in twos, heartily cheered on our way by the inhabitants of Camden Town. We stood on the station platform feeling rather subdued. At last the train came and we bundled in. Only the engine driver knew our destination.

Mum's last words rang in my ears. 'Write soon and look after Rosemary.' Who's going to look after me I thought.

My father's funeral was the same day that my three sisters, my brother and I were evacuated. We all looked out of the bedroom window and watched the funeral cars depart, then we gathered up our bundles and went to our school.

In the case of this group there were no tearful farewells. We were already many miles from our parents, and we were with our friends. We travelled in two charabancs, taking with us a few members of staff and one of the joint headmistresses. We were bound for Woolacombe, a holiday resort in North Devon, which was an idyllic situation . . . There are three miles of sand at Woolacombe and swimming would be much more interesting than it is in the swimming pool at Reigate.

I remember asking Lila, my sister's friend, why all the people were standing in their gardens waving to us, and she said, 'They feel sorry for us. Try to cry, to make it worthwhile'.

What excitement, what a scurry
Tying labels in a hurry,
Mother shouting from the stairs,
'Have you got your socks in pairs?'
Haversacks full to the brim,
Clothes all folded neat and trim,
Round each neck is tied a label,
To tell who's 'Joan' and who is 'Mabel'.

QUESTIONS *to think and talk about*

- Which of these memories do you think would fit Kim's school, and which the boarding school?
- Do the writers feel the same way about being evacuated? How are they different from each other?
- Out of all the memories printed above, which one do you like the most? Which one do you think is the most moving?
- What is the longest journey you have been on?
- How did you travel? Would Kim have travelled as you did?
- Do you remember a time when you were frightened of travelling?

Compare your knowledge about Britain and about travelling with these three memories.

As the train started moving forward, there was a mighty roar from every compartment which could be heard for miles, as the train was so full it was bursting at the seams. After about half an hour, though, the whole train went dead quiet, for on looking out of the window, everything had suddenly turned green . . . How much further, I thought, could it go before the train fell off the coast of Scotland into the sea? For even at this young age I knew Scotland ended at water's edge somewhere or other.

I can remember, though, how we had to cross a viaduct, how frightened we all were in case the train should come off the rails and we should all fall into the water underneath. You should have heard the sighs of relief when we crossed safely.

I sat with my eyes tightly closed in fear, and it seemed every time I opened them I was surrounded by nothing but mountains and

> very strange animals I had never seen before. There were so many of these strange creatures I felt they would at any time gang together to attack the train and devour all the passengers. It was a good while later I discovered they were sheep.

TASKS

I Set up your class or drama room in a way that represents an evacuees' train. As a group, discuss:
– What the evacuees would see from the windows and their reactions;
– The sorts of things the evacuees would be doing on the train and the general atmosphere.

After five minutes of discussing the scene in this way, imagine that *you* are the evacuees and bring the scene to life. Keep the improvisation going for at least five minutes.

You may choose to have two railway guards in the carriage: one is friendly and trying to make the journey interesting for the evacuees by pointing things out to them; the other is mainly concerned with preventing the children from misbehaving.

Discuss how well you think the improvisation captured the details and atmosphere of the situation.

2 Work in small groups. Choose five particular moments that you think an evacuee would remember about her or his journey. Make a tableau for each one. Find a way of linking the five pictures together by using a narrator. The 'story' can be told by someone in the pictures, or someone on the outside looking at the pictures.

3 During a quiet moment on the journey, some of the evacuees write postcards. In role as an evacuee, write a card to someone at home.

Some children were evacuated by boat. To many city children, this must have been even more exciting, or terrifying, than going on a train or bus. Some children were taken as far away as Canada, though this was stopped after one of the ships carrying evacuees was torpedoed. Some children had a rather disappointing experience:

> 'After what seemed like hours of stopping, then starting, we arrived at our final destination. We had expected green fields and trees. What we got was Luton.'

At the end of Kim's story, she says that no-one cheers when the train moves again after being stuck in a siding. Look at the picture on p. 21 and imagine that this is one of the children on Kim's train. What do you think he is thinking about?

4   Imagine that you are the adult who looks after the little boy in this photograph. As you said goodbye to him, you slipped a letter into his pocket – just as Kim's father did. What does it say?

5   How could you show what children and adults separated by the evacuation are thinking and feeling about each other? Divide into small groups and decide who in the family you are. Make a tableau which shows who is who. Try to alter the tableau to show your relationship to each other. Are the children, for example, closer to their mother or father? Are the children jealous of each other? How can you show what they normally feel? Alter the picture once more to show how they feel about the evacuation. You may need to use more space to capture their separation.

If each character could say one line which sums up their feelings about the situation, what would they say?

6   What instructions might an evacuee leave behind for the people he or she lives with to follow?

7   Rewrite the words of a popular song that the evacuees might have sung to keep their spirits up. Here is an example of one that was sung at the time:

Whistle while you work
Goering is a berk
Hitler's barmy
So's his army
Whistle while you work.

Ask some adults you know if they know any of the songs that were popular during the War.

Mrs Peacock: A TEACHER'S TALE . . . .

Most children were evacuated with all their schoolmates. Their teachers went with them – to carry on teaching them and to help find them new homes.

What sort of problems did the teachers have to deal with?

What was it like, having the responsibility of helping others in this situation?

This letter, and the work that follows, will give you some idea about the sort of pressures that were felt by those with responsibility.

Playtime. To continue . . .

No doubt some will say how the whole operation is a tremendous success. It's not, of course – it's an utter shambles. I'm told, for example, that most of London's pregnant women have been sent together to St Alban's. Some man's idea of efficiency, I suppose!

As for us, we were told that posters had been put up all over the countryside to try to attract people to help out. There would be no shortage of volunteers to put everyone up, they said. Ha! The rate paid by the government for putting evacuees up isn't terribly good. No doubt some people will accept lots of evacuees just to get the money, but how well will they be looked after? No doubt we shall find out soon enough.

The moment I arrived here I could see that no real organisation existed for dealing with us. Some of the village women have done their utmost to help, of course. The school and some other hall-like buildings have been opened up for us to stay in for the time being, but there are no blankets, no fires and very little in the way of food.

One kind farmer placed his cart at our disposal and we took groups of the children around the outlying villages. At each stop, the locals would come out and look over our sorry cargo and pick the ones they were prepared to take. Naturally, they picked the cleanest and best kept, or those that looked as if they'd be able to earn their keep. We were out till gone midnight, with one little boy left. You can no doubt imagine how he must have been feeling. I can't honestly say that he has ever been my favourite pupil, but even so . . .

We've given all the children a postcard to send home as soon as they know their new address. One says:
'Dear Mum, I hope you are well. I don't like the man's face much. Perhaps it will look better in daylight. I like the dog's face best.'

Some of the children certainly seem to have fallen on their feet, though, and will be better cared for here than they were at home. Certainly, the fresh air and open spaces will do them the world of good, as will the fresh vegetables and other foodstuffs available here. Not surprisingly, though, some of the children are very unhappy. Many more are still in a state of awe at their billets and surroundings. We have some who have come from the poorest of homes in the city and who are billeted in a mansion. They've come from houses where it is quite common to sleep five or six to a bed and, frankly, their level of hygiene isn't all it could be.

I can see some big problems looming on the horizon. Some of the locals seem to regard them as a bit of a novelty. Others are openly hostile, and some of our lads have already been in fights. The situation in the school is hardly helping matters. It only has one classroom and must have been barely adequate before. Now we have five classes in there instead of the two it's used to. Getting everybody settled into their place is a nightmare. We've set up two blackboards, one at each end of the room. The largest blackboard is divided into three sections, the smaller into two. Can you imagine us five teachers whispering desperately to our pupils, trying to persuade them to concentrate? The only other room in the building is home to five bicycles and all of the children's and teachers' clothes. The roof and gutters leak dismally. A cascade pours over the entrance and exit to the school where the gutter has entirely collapsed.

So far this morning, three of us have vile headaches and the other two are just thoroughly fed up. The postman told us that the classroom floor has collapsed under all the extra weight in the next village. I'm so pleased that he thought it was funny!

This afternoon, I shall try to find homes for the last few. I must also try to find out where young Peter Winskill has disappeared to. There was 'an incident' yesterday with some of the local boys and he hasn't been seen since.

There's the bell. Once more unto the breach . . .

Will continue this later.

QUESTIONS *to think and talk about*

- How long do you think Mrs Peacock has been away from her normal home?
- What is her attitude to the evacuation so far?
- Who might she be writing to?
- If you were in Mrs Peacock's situation, which problem would you find hardest to handle?

TASKS

1   Look back through Mrs Peacock's story and note down at least five phrases which you think could be used for a scene to act out. For example, 'The postman told us that the classroom floor has collapsed under all the extra weight in the next village'.

In pairs, or small groups, choose just one of the phrases that you have picked out. Invent some other scenes that might happen *because* of it. Set out your ideas on a sheet of paper like this:

The head complains to a local official about conditions.

A local child blames an evacuee for causing the damage.

The floor collapses in the middle of a lesson.

An evacuated teacher tries to persuade a farmer to let her class use his barn for lessons

An evacuee who has come from a good, modern school in the city, tells her parents about the incident when they visit.

In what order would you put your scenes, to make a play about the arrival of the evacuees in the country? Either write or improvise a short play based on your ideas.

2   How would you play out the scene in which the classroom floor collapses? Work in small groups to experiment. What different effects are created by doing it in different ways? For example, does it always look funny, or can it be done in a way that shows how hard the situation was for those involved?

Can it be done just in movement, or just in words? Decide on what you think is the best way, and, after rehearsing it, compare your version with other groups.

3   As a whole class, set up a meeting in which local and evacuated teachers talk about the problems they are having. Decide what sort of teacher you are. Use Mrs Peacock's letter, and the scenes you devised, as examples of the problems you might be having. What do the teachers decide to do? How will they try to carry out their plans?

4   Mrs Peacock says that she intends to finish the letter later. Using clues from what she has already said, write the end of the letter for her.

PREPARING THE HOSTS

This is one of the posters that was put up in villages and country towns during the summer of 1939. Its aim was to get people to volunteer to put up evacuees, should war break out.

Who'll give a promise to keep this child safe?

This child's home is in the city. Up to the present his home has been safe. But let us face it : one of these days his home may be a ruin. There is no excuse for feeling falsely secure because nothing has happened yet. The danger of air-raids is as great now as it has ever been.

The Government is arranging to send this child, and some hundred thousands of others, to safety if raiders come. Each will need a home. Only one household in five is caring for these children now. Volunteers are urgently needed. Plans must be made well ahead. There must be no hitch, no delay, in settling the children in safety. Here is *your* chance to help.

You can if you wish make an immediate contribution to this safety scheme. Many households have been looking after evacuated children for six months now. They will be grateful for a rest. If you can take over one of these children, you will be doing a very neighbourly deed and helping greatly in the nation's defence.

To enrol as a host of a child now or in the future, or to ask any questions about the scheme, please get in touch with your local Authority.

The Minister of Health, who has been entrusted by the Government with the conduct of evacuation, asks you urgently to join the Roll of those who are willing to receive children. Please apply to your local Council.

A survey had found that four and a half million evacuees could be housed in the country. This figure was based on the idea of each evacuee having a room of her or his own. In theory, there should have been no problem finding rooms for the three and a half million mothers and children who were evacuated. In practice, it was much harder.

In 1939, the average wage for a working person was between £2–3 per week. Look at the chart below, which shows what hosts were being offered to house an evacuee.

Allowances to householders

For children not accompanied by adults (full board and lodging) :
10s 6d ($52\frac{1}{2}$p) per week for the first child
8s 6d ($42\frac{1}{2}$p) per week for each additional child

For mothers with children (lodging only) :
5s (25p) per week for adults
3s (15p) per week for children

For teachers and helpers (lodging only) :
5s (25p) per week

The allowances were raised in 1940, and the rates for children were based on their age.

QUESTIONS *to think and talk about*

- Why do you think so many people were reluctant to put up evacuees?
- In what ways do you think country people expected town people to be different from themselves?
- What sort of child do you think would be the easiest to look after?

When the evacuees arrived in the country, though, not all of them found a warm welcome:

We felt like cattle at an auction, when one of the remaining ladies – who looked rather forbidding – was spoken to by an official and later declared, 'All right, I'll take these two'.

A friend of mine had two little girls and she was picked out by this farmer . . . he lived in a derelict cottage. He told her the children would sleep on the settee and she'd sleep with him. She came back the same night.

Six evacuees, they had. Listen how many rooms they had! They had three bedrooms and a front room. Six evacuees, three of their own, and themselves. Us evacuees more or less slept in the same room. He was doing it for the money.

If you were similar to Shirley Temple, you were grabbed right away.

TASKS

1 In pairs, work on one of these scenes:

(*a*) A is a billeting officer, desperate to find homes. He or she is trying to persuade B to take an evacuee. What arguments does A use to persuade B?

(*b*) B is a local person who seems very keen to take in a number of evacuees. A is a billeting officer who is rather suspicious of B's motives. How does A find out why B wants so many?

(*c*) A is a billeting officer, B a local person. B is very happy to take in an evacuee, but there is one problem! What is the problem that B presents, and how does A cope with it?

2 If you were responsible for the housing of evacuees in your own area, what advice would you give to your team of billeting officers? Write a leaflet which will introduce them to the problems of the area.

3 As a whole class, devise a pamphlet to welcome the evacuees to the area. Decide first of all who might contribute to such a pamphlet: the local vicar, the squire, shopkeepers, a farmer, the leader of the Brownie pack, etc., and write each of your pieces accordingly.

FINDING HOMES

Look carefully at the photograph below.

– Look at the expressions on the people's faces.
– Look at the clothes they are wearing.
– Look at the bit of the house shown.

QUESTIONS *to think and talk about*

For these questions, you will need to make some guesses, but the photograph will give you clues.

• What do you think it shows happening?

• Try to describe what you think the children are feeling by the looks on their faces.

• Who's who in this picture?

- What do you think is the attitude of the two adults in the background towards the children?
- What sort of house do you suppose this is? How big is it? In what sort of area?

Now look at this picture:

- What are the differences between the way the little girl at the bottom left-hand corner is dressed and the way the children in the group are dressed? What does this tell you?
- How easy do you think staying in this house would have been for these evacuees?

TASKS

1 In small groups, position yourselves like the people in the first photograph. What do you think they could be saying? Continue the scene for just one or two minutes, discuss what you have done, then choose the five most appropriate lines for this picture. Get back into position and say the chosen lines in an appropriate way. Share your work, and discuss whether the atmosphere is different in each version.

2 In pairs, or small groups, act out a scene in which someone who lives in the manor house in the second photograph shows the evacuees around. That person could be the master of the house, or a servant. What 'dos' and 'don'ts' have to be explained?

What sort of questions do the evacuees ask as they are shown around?

Now read this extract from a novel about the Second World War called *The Dolphin Crossing*.

The Dolphin Crossing

He spoke in Welsh, urgently. They looked out at us, peering into the darkness from their doorways, looking us over. We couldn't understand a word, yet it was easy to tell whether they were saying yes or no. Several times the man pushed me forwards, and the woman shook her head, and said something, and took a small child, much younger. I was nearly full grown by then, head and shoulders taller than the others in the group. At last I was the only one left, and he scratched his head a bit, and then took me up a rough track, still uphill, on and on, and then when I thought I couldn't walk a step further, he brought me through a yard of some kind, and knocked on a door. The woman who came said no, like all the others when she saw me, but he talked and talked, and then a man came to the door too, and joined in. Then suddenly the man who had brought me from the station left, and trudged away down the hillside, and they let me in through their door.

It was a big farm kitchen I walked into. A great log fire was burning in the chimney corner, and there was bread and cheese, and a cold roast chicken on the table. I was so hungry the sight of food made me feel tight in the stomach. They looked at me and the man said something in Welsh.

'How old is it you are?' she asked me, in English.

'Fifteen,' I said.

'You look more. I thought you were a grown man when you stood out in the dark there,' she said. 'Will you want your bed right away?'

'Can I have something to eat first?' I asked.

'Right away, boy. Sit down then,' she said. She put food in front of me, four sorts of bread, and great hunks of cheese, and butter with beads of saltwater shining in it, and the rest of the chicken. She sat down by the hearth, and folded her hands in her lap, and the two of them talked together in Welsh. I listened to all that musical mumbo-jumbo and ate and ate, and as soon as I stopped feeling hungry my head dropped forwards onto my hands, and I fell asleep at the table where I sat.

– Where does the incident take place?
– What do we know about the person who is telling the story?
– Why do you think people are so reluctant to take him in?

Read the extract again. What details does the storyteller seem to notice about his new home? What might this tell us about the one he has left behind?

TASKS

3 In threes, try to act out the scene in the farm kitchen. The person telling the story obviously feels very out of place. How can you show this? What do you suppose the Welsh couple are saying, knowing that the boy can't understand them? You may wish them to talk in English for the purpose of your scene.

4 In small groups, make up a scene of your own which shows how and why an evacuee feels very out of place on her/his first night away from home.

5 Imagine that you are the boy in the extract. Write a letter to a friend, or your parents, describing your new home and the surrounding countryside.

SETTLING IN

The memories below show that finding a new home was a different experience for different people:

They wanted a little girl with M.G. as initials because their sports car had M.G. on the bumper.

One lady chose Teddy, and as he started to climb down, clutching his little cardboard case, she saw a set of twins and said, 'Oh, no. I've changed my mind, I'd sooner have them'. Poor Teddy had to climb back up and ended up being the last one left.

Out came a lady wearing corduroy trousers! This was a shock because I had never seen a female in trousers before.

She was the same age and exactly like the daughter they had lost, and they took her back to their house and even the dog went mad with happiness.

Later, in a strange cold bed at the end of that long, weary day, I hid under the bedclothes and cried. Then I remembered that we hadn't said our prayers, and with this as an excuse, I climbed into my brother's bed while he said, 'Gentle Jesus . . .'.

At the end of our prayers we curled up together and my little five-year-old brother said, 'Don't cry, Jean, I'll look after you'.

Not all evacuated children had bad experiences. One evacuee has said:

I thank God I was evacuated: not because I avoided danger, which was the purpose of the evacuation, but because it changed my way of thinking. It made me love the country: I could never live in town again. When I look back to those days, I know I found a refuge, quiet and peaceful, after an unhappy home life: I found another family whom I really loved, and still do.

TASKS

1   Mrs Peacock says that once homes had been found for all the children, they were told to send a postcard to their parents. Imagine that you are an evacuee. What would you write to your parents on a postcard? If you could draw on the blank side, showing what you have found most surprising about your new home, what would you draw?

2   As a whole class, imagine that you are all teachers from various schools which have just been evacuated. How would you set up a meeting, in order to discuss the problems you

have had so far, and what you think should happen next?

3 If you were a teacher, like Mrs Peacock, what problems would you see ahead of you? Write an entry in a personal diary, explaining your fears.

4 If you were the last child to be chosen off the cart, what would be going through your mind? Write down your thoughts, and try to shape what you have written into a poem, called – for example – 'Last To Go'.

5 In small groups, find a way of presenting some of your poems. What sort of images would match feelings in them? What tone and volume of voice would be most appropriate for the reading?

The old man in this picture seems popular with the children. Why do you think this is?

Invent a character for the man and some details about his life. For example:

– How old is he?
– What is his name?

– Where does he live?
– What is his house like?
– What skills does he teach the children?
– What stories does he tell them?

TASKS

1 Choose a member of the class to take on the role of the old man and 'hot-seat' him, in order to find out more details about his life and his attitude towards the evacuees.

2 Draw a picture of the old man's sitting room and describe in detail some of his most special possessions.

3 In pairs, or small groups, make up a scene which shows why this old man became so popular with the evacuees in his village.

PROBLEMS

In Mrs Peacock's story, we hear that she can see 'big problems' ahead. Look carefully at these memories below. They hint at different kinds of problems.

The village didn't know what hit them when we first arrived, it was gang warfare between us and the local kids. There wasn't a fruit tree within miles around with a single item of fruit left on it.

I don't know which I dreaded more, meeting a herd of cows in the lane home, or being cornered by a bunch of local boys.

Rose has been whispering since we got here. Everything is so clean in the room. We've been given flannels and toothbrushes. We've never cleaned our teeth up till now. There's a lavatory upstairs and carpets. And something called an eiderdown, and clean sheets, and it's all rather scary.

We didn't know anything about nature and we ran after the peacocks and tore the tail feathers from them to send home to our mum.

The country is a funny place. They never tell you you can't have no more to eat, and under the bed is wasted.

How I wish the prevalent view of the evacuees could be changed. We were not all raised on a diet of fish and chips eaten from newspaper, and many of us were quite familiar with the origins of milk! It was just as traumatic for a clean and fairly well-educated child to find itself in a grubby semi-slum as *vice versa*.

We went under the Government scheme and came from very respectable homes. Some of the girls ended up in tiny cottages, three to a single bed, with bedbugs – which they had never seen in their lives. I wasn't allowed to wash my hair for four months, since we had to bring the water up a hill from the village pump.

I said to her, 'We've got clean heads, what are you looking for?' and she said, 'I'm looking for your horns'.

(Rita Friede, a Jewish girl.)

I was forced to share the bed with an incontinent Yorkshire ten-year-old called 'Ower George'. 'Ower George' became such a bore, with his football and bed-wetting, that I was finally obliged to turn him over to the form bully, who had, thankfully, travelled north with us.

A few of the hosts. . .treated their evacuees, who were mainly girls, as guests, or as they would their own children; but the majority treated the girls as unpaid maids.

Just as some of the country's poorest city children found themselves staying in comfortable, clean homes, other children from city suburbs (outskirts) were amazed and appalled by what life was like in the countryside. Many villages at the time did not have electricity or running water in the homes. Life for farm labourers was hard. Some of the country folk were ignorant and prejudiced.

This picture shows how some farm labourers in Kent lived just fifty years ago.

TASKS

1 In pairs, or small groups, improvise one of these scenes.

(a) A is an evacuee from a rather well-off home. She has been billeted with a poor farm labourer who expects her to repay his hospitality by doing the housework and helping in the yard. She wants to get on with her school studies. One evening, he arrives home to find her reading a book. She hasn't cooked his meal as he told her to. What happens?

(*b*) An evacuee's parent visits her child and is disgusted at the conditions in the host's home. Act out the scene between the parent and the host. What are their attitudes towards each other? Do they make their feelings known, or do they remain polite?

(*c*) An evacuee from a poor background has been put in a very rich house. When the evacuee's parent visits for the first time, the host is very hostile. The host makes it clear that he or she doesn't think the parent very responsible since the child was so shabbily dressed and badly fed when he or she arrived. What is the parent's reaction?

2 Use any one of the memories printed on p. 34-35 as the starting point for a scene of your own. Share your work. The scenes should show:
- a particular problem faced by the evacuees;
- where the problem came from;
- how those involved react to the problem.

SCHOOL LIFE

In 1939, most children left school when they were fourteen years old. In many villages, the school had just one main schoolroom in which all children between the ages of five and fourteen were taught.

Is there an old school near to you? (Perhaps you are in one, or went to one). Find out how old the school is and whether it was evacuated, or accommodated evacuees.

All schools keep a 'log book', which notes down the major events of each day. Some old schools may still have their log books from the war years. Try to find out if an old school in your area has its log book for the years 1939–45. The headteacher will certainly know. They are fascinating and may well hold some interesting stories which will be worth investigating.

Standards of education in the 1930s varied greatly, and attitudes towards pupils were often harsh. The arrival of the evacuees put a great strain on everyone and teachers didn't always handle the new problems very well:

> My most unpleasant memory is of one little evacuee being caned in front of my class at school because he had run away from his temporary home three times. As I sat and had to watch, I thought how very stupid adults are, even headmasters – instead of finding

out why the boy was so unhappy as to run away, to make him much more so by punishment. I regret to this day, not having the courage of my convictions to protest, or to comfort this unfortunate boy, who sat at the back of the class.

Look carefully at this picture of a wartime schoolroom:

- What can you see in the photograph that tells you it was taken during the War?

- What differences are there between this and your own classroom?

Find out from elderly people that you know what they remember about their schooldays. What subjects did they do? How did the teachers treat them?

TASKS

1 Set up your classroom as you think it would have looked in 1939. In pairs, describe any other details that would be different: for example, what might be on the walls? What sort of work would you be doing? What would you be writing with?

As a whole class, decide how a typical lesson in 1939 would have been carried out. Act out those bits of the lesson that show the main differences. Try to capture what you think is the right atmosphere.

2 In Mrs Peacock's story, we hear that one child has gone missing. In the memories printed above, we hear of another runaway who was severely punished. In small groups, make up a short play about two evacuees who want to run away. They try to persuade their friends to go with them. How do they do this? Are their friends persuaded, or do they have reasons for not wanting to go? Show what decision is reached and what happens next.

3 Imagine that the Headmaster who punished the runaway was made to face a Board of Enquiry. Set up the scene in which he explains his actions to them.

4 Write the end-of-term report for a child who has been evacuated, or, in pairs, improvise the scene in which a teacher goes through the report with the pupil.

LESLEY: A HOST'S TALE ·························

You may already know how hard it is to share your home and possessions. Perhaps you have a relative who sometimes comes to stay and 'spoils everything'?

But what if someone like that came and didn't go home again? An evacuee, for example?

What if they were different from you in their attitudes and habits? What sacrifices would you be willing to make for such a visitor?

The diary below traces one girl's reaction to the arrival of the evacuees in her home.

September 20th 1939

Dear Diary,
 Now the War has really broken out! I don't mean between the British and the Germans (see Sept. 3rd for news of that). This war is between us 'yokels' and the 'townees'. If the last few days are anything to go by, I should think we'll end up killing each other well before Hitler gets here.
 If you say two words to some of them, they turn around and swear at you. Marjorie Brown's two have carved their initials on the sideboard, and scribbled on the walls. They eat their food – and even sleep – on the floor. Worse still, Marjorie says they piddle on the walls.
 Thank goodness we haven't got any!

September 27th 1939

Dear Diary,
 Hmmmm! Mum says we're taking in two 'vacuees'. I don't know where they're from, why we've got them or where they are going to sleep. They're not coming in this room, that's for sure.

October 4th 1939

Dear Diary,
 'THEY' have arrived. A girl aged thirteen (called Sheila) and her monster brother aged four (Vincent). He bit me! I don't think he'll do it again, though, because I bit him back.

This diary lives in a locked drawer from now on! In fact, I suggested to Mum that we lock everything that can be moved away (or lock THEM in the shed).

October 10th 1939

Dear Diary,

Excellent chance to put the Townees in their place today. All the top class had to go up to the farm to help with the harvest. Normally, I hate going, but today was wonderful. The Townees hadn't a clue. Two of the boys (trying to show off, of course) said they wanted to milk the cows. One put the pail under the cow's udders and was holding it there while the other boy was using the cow's tail like a pump handle! Our own dear Sheila's eyes nearly popped out when she saw the geese. I told her they were man-eating sparrows, only found here in Kent.

Monkeys would have been more use stacking the hay! Life isn't so bad, after all, with entertainment like that free of charge.

October 17th 1939

Dear Diary,

Sent to bed early, thanks to Mother's sense of justice. I came home black and blue after the rotten 'vacuees got their revenge for the farm trip and dear Mother took their side! Just because both Snivelling Sheila and Vicious Vincent erupted in tears about how nasty I am to them. Nasty? I don't talk to them, so how can I be nasty?

P.S.   Mum has had a chat with me. No need to give details. She has a point, I suppose.

P.P.S   Sheila crept in late and actually said she was sorry that she'd hit me. It's about the first time she's said anything to me. I said sorry back. I suppose she's all right, really. I wouldn't like to be responsible for Vincent the Vile, like she has to be.

November 6th 1939

Dear Diary,

Sheila and Vince's mum and dad turned up to see them. I don't know who I feel sorry for most. Vince is just like his dad – violent, foulmouthed, ignorant.

Sheila stayed quiet. I think she was a bit embarrassed of them. She told me afterwards that her mum might take her back to London soon, to help in the house when the new baby arrives (I hope it's more like Sheila than Virus Vincent). Loads of the vacuees are going back for Christmas. Lots of them say they're going back for good. There are posters everywhere telling them not to, but you can see why they are.

December 26th 1939

Dear Diary,

Happy Christmas. Ha, ha! Well, we all tried. Poor Sheila. I even felt sorry for Vince. Not a single present from their mum and dad. Not even a card. Nothing.

Lots of special things going on this year in the village. Everyone really pulled together. With so many people having a good time, it must have felt even worse for Sheila and Vince.

August 3rd 1940

Dear Diary,

Our very own air-raid shelter arrived today. Since Dunkirk, they've been springing up everywhere. A brick one is being built in the School playground, and the farm workers have dug slit trenches in most of the fields. Dad and Mr Harpwood have spent all day digging it in and banking up earth around the outside. When we've got a fire and the bunk beds in, it'll be quite cosy.

It's all quite exciting, really. I still haven't seen a German bomber yet, though a Spitfire went over the playground yesterday and the pilot waved at us. Still no news from Sheila's mum about how Vince is getting on back home. I quite miss him, really, though I suppose I'm glad it's him that went back and not Sheila.

August 11th 1940

Dear Diary,

Air-raid practice has taken over from gas-mask drill as Public Nuisance Number One. In and out of the classroom all day long. We miss lots of lessons, though the siren only ever seems to go in the good ones. The shelter is cramped, damp and uncomfortable. If anyone makes a joke, the Head says, 'War is not a laughing matter'. He's telling me!

September 15th 1940

Dear Diary,

Charlie Cummins heard that both his parents and his eldest sister are dead today. Sheila was really nice to him. I didn't realise they were cousins. Bombing in London is very bad. We can hear it at night, and even see the glow of the fires in the sky.

Vince has been sent away again. This time to Wales. (God help the mountain goats!)

Another dog fight overhead this afternoon. No warning this time, so we got a good look before being shooed into the stinking rotten shelter. Why they evacuated anyone here in the first place, I don't know. We'll all be moving out soon if the raids go on like this. We spend most nights in the shelter, listening to the bombers going over. At least the nights are quite warm just now. It's going to be awful when the winter comes.

July 18th 1941

Dear Diary,

Boring, boring, boring, boring, boring.

Fed up with rotten rationing. My clothes are dreadful. Mystery pie for tea again. God knows what Mum puts in it. She doesn't say and I don't like to ask.

Fed up with school, though what I'll do when I leave, I don't know.

Fed up with not hearing from Sheila. You'd think she could at least have written. It's been three months since she went home. I know she's not dead or anything. London hasn't been hit for ages. What could have happened to her?

I wonder if we'll ever meet again.

QUESTIONS *to think and talk about*

- What sort of person is Lesley? How would you describe her?
- Do you think she has any brothers or sisters?
- What sort of house do you imagine she lives in?
- In what ways does she change in the time covered by these diary extracts?
- What do you think might have happened to Vincent and Sheila?

TASKS

1 Imagine that a film is going to be made, in which Lesley is the main character. Write some notes about her, which will help the actress playing the part.

2 In pairs, improvise one of these scenes.

(*a*) One of Lesley's parents is called to talk to her teacher about the incident at the farm.

(*b*) Mum has a 'chat' with Lesley about her treatment of Sheila and Vince.

(*c*) Sheila apologises for hitting Lesley and they talk openly for the first time.

(*d*) Lesley's parents talk to each other after Sheila's parents have visited.

3 In small groups, choose five things which you think would have helped to change Lesley's character during the War. The incidents may come from the diary extracts, or you can invent them yourself.

Make a still image for each one, which clearly shows how and why this moment is important for Lesley. Find a way of linking the five images together. If you need to use words, keep them down to a minimum. Try to rely on movement and expression to suggest what is happening to Lesley.

4 What do you think Sheila is like as a person? How would she write about her stay with Lesley in a diary?

5 In small groups, devise a scene in which Lesley and Sheila eventually meet up again. What memories do they share? Experiment with the idea of 'flashbacks', as a way of showing what they are remembering.

DIFFERENT WORLDS

City and country people at that time generally knew very little about each other's way of life. Ordinary people didn't travel as much then as they do now, so the chance of meeting people who lived very differently was quite small. Even if they knew little, though, they probably *expected* certain things of each other.

QUESTIONS *to think and talk about*

- What differences are there between the children in Lesley's village and the 'townees'?

- Lesley says that 'war' has broken out between them. What sort of things might have happened for her to say that?

Lesley obviously enjoyed teasing the 'townees' about how little they knew of country life. The piece of writing opposite was broadcast by the BBC shortly after the evacuation:

The cow is a mamal. It has six sides, right, left and upper and below. At the back it has a tail, on which hangs a brush. With this it sends the flies away so they do not fall into the milk. The head is for the purpose of growing horns and so that the mouth can be somewhere. The horns are to butt with and the mouth is to moo with. Under the cow hangs the milk. It is arranged for milking. When people milk, the milk comes and there is never an end to the supply. How the cow does it 1 have not yet realised, but it makes more and more. The cow has a fine sense of smell, one can smell it far away. This is the reason for the fresh air in the country.

The man cow is called an ox. It is not a mamal. The cow does not eat much, but what it eats its eats twice, so that it gets enough. When it is hungry it moos and when it says nothing, it is because all the inside is full up with grass.

- What would you think about this piece if you were Lesley, or one of her friends in the village?
- What would your reaction have been to it if you were one of the 'vacuees' who had been to the farm with Lesley that day?

TASKS

1 In pairs, think of something that might cause friction between the 'townees' and the 'yokels' (for example, the visit to the farm). Write your idea on a card and swop the cards around within the class.

Use the idea on the card you have been given as the basis for these interviews:

(*a*) A is a host, B is a reporter from the local paper who is writing an article about the effect the evacuees are having on the town. B asks A to give as many details as possible about recent incidents concerning the evacuees.

(*b*) B is an evacuee, A becomes the reporter and tries to find out the other side of the story.

(*c*) A is the parent of an evacuee, B the parent of a local child. What would they say to each other about the incident?

2 Imagine that you write for BBC radio programmes during the War. You have been asked to come up with something about the evacuation that will cheer people up. Work on your own, or in pairs, to produce a short radio programme. You could include poems, short stories or reports of incidents concerned with the evacuation. Any of the material in this book could be used, or you could make up your own material (it is most likely that the piece called 'The Cow is a Mamal' was, in fact, made up).

If you were to record your radio programme, try to find a suitable piece of music to use as an introduction.

3 As a whole class, imagine that you are the people who decide whether or not to broadcast these programmes. Listen to the recordings and discuss the effects they would have on:
– those who have been evacuated;
– parents of evacuees;
– host families;
– the relations between evacuees and hosts.
Would these programmes cheer people up, or cause more friction?

4 As a class, discuss the way people from different areas are 'stereotyped' today. Are people from your area always shown on television as talking or behaving in a particular way? Do you think this kind of characterisation is acceptable?

THE PHONEY WAR ENDS

After the War broke out in September 1939, very little seemed to happen. People started to call it 'the Phoney War'. As Christmas drew near, many children, and even more of the mothers, decided to return home to the cities. Some of them probably went back because they couldn't get on with country life and country people; others because they missed their own homes and families.

Just four months after the evacuation plan was put into operation, 88% of all mothers evacuated, and 86% of the children, had returned home – even though the Government had launched a campaign to keep them in the safety of the countryside.

This is one of the posters you might have seen on village noticeboards:

TASKS

1   Design a poster of your own, warning against taking children back to the cities.

2   You have probably seen Public Information films on television about, for example, the dangers of smoking or drinking and driving. In small groups, imagine that you are film-makers in 1940 and the Government has asked you to make a short film to prevent parents taking their children back to the cities. Prepare a specimen scene for them to review.

Share the scenes, and consider what effect each would have on parents of evacuated children.

3   Having listened to some comments about your scene, produce a storyboard for the rest of the film by dividing a sheet of paper into eight squares. Think of your film as a cartoon and use simple stick-people drawings to show the most important moments of the film. Any speech, or special instruction, should be noted beneath each picture like this:

Mum : Come on, children. It's time I was going.

Boy : But mummy we hate it here. We don't know anyone
Girl : Pees us come back you Mummy?

Bombs being loaded onto German Bombers
Boys Voice : Yes, please Mummy. We'll be safe with you.

Inside Bomber Cockpit Close up of map showing London
Girl Voice: Me like Lonnon best, Mummy

Bombers flying in evening sky
Boy + Girl Please Mummy Please.

Mum : I know it's difficult children but you must trust me...

Country lane
.... I'll speak to Mrs Smith. It'll be allright

Churchill:
"That's right, Mum Keep them where they're safe"

4 In pairs, A is a parent who has seen the posters and films but has still decided to take the children home. B is a representative from the Government's film unit who is trying to find out why the publicity has failed.

5 As a whole class, divide yourselves into evacuees and hosts. Imagine that you have been called to a meeting at which a Government official is to speak about the dangers of going back to the cities. How do you feel about this? Do you think the evacuees should stay or go?

Set up your room as if it were a village hall, and improvise the meeting.

In the Spring of 1940, the German army was advancing quickly towards the Channel. The British army was trapped on the beach at Dunkirk, in Northern France, and had to be hurriedly evacuated back to Britain. It became obvious that Britain was to be the next stop on Hitler's travels!

In August 1940, battles were fought daily in the skies over Southern Britain. The long-expected bombing finally started, and although most attacks were on the big cities, many country towns and villages were hit by lone bombers on 'hit-and-run' raids. Sometimes, if the bombers were being attacked by RAF fighters, they would hastily get rid of their bombs and try to escape:

> It was ironic, to say the least – us being evacuated to such a beautiful and peaceful place – as the local school received a direct hit from a stray German plane. All forty-eight children and teachers lost their lives.

TASKS

1 How can you show what happened to this school through drama? One way is to choose a number of key moments – rather like the storyboard idea – and then link them together.

Key moments in this scene might show:
- the class at work;
- they hear distant gunfire and bombing;
- they realise an aircraft is approaching;
- they try to take cover;

— explosions followed by stillness. Your work may be more effective if, instead of rushing around screaming, you find a way of slowing down the action and use movement and gesture to capture the feelings. Experiment with your voices, or some percussion instruments, to make a soundtrack which fits your scene.

2   Imagine that you are a local person who has rushed to the school immediately after the raid. Jot down some words and phrases that describe what you see and feel.

Arrange your notes into a poem. You could call it 'Last Lesson of the Day', or 'Hit and Run'.

3   In small groups, imagine that you are searching the rubble for survivors. The building is very unsafe – any sudden movements or loud noises could cause more sections to cave in. Move carefully, and listen for noises which could tell you where survivors are buried. Suddenly, you think you hear a child crying. Carry on the scene.

AIR-RAIDS AND SHELTERS

Concrete and brick shelters were built in many school playgrounds. Households were issued with 'Anderson' shelters. These often had to be shared with neighbours.

If you live in a country area, find out if there were any 'hit-and-run' incidents locally during the War.

After the War, many people kept their Anderson shelters as sheds. You can still see them on garden allotments. School shelters can be found in some playgrounds. They are often used as equipment stores.

QUESTIONS *to think and talk about*

Overleaf are some pictures of different types of shelter. Take a careful look at each one.

- Has the picture been taken before, during or after a raid? Perhaps the people are just practising?
- What sort of area is the shelter in? Town, country or suburb?
- What sort of feelings do you think the people in each picture have about their shelter and the situation they are in? Are they frightened, excited, fed up?

When the bombing started at the end of 1940, a second evacuation was put into operation. Many mothers and children took a chance and stayed in their city homes. Many of them were killed. Between September and November 1940, three million homes were damaged or destroyed; 30,000 people were killed.

This extract is from Robert Westall's book, *The Machine Gunners*. It describes what life in the Blitz was like:

Early Evening Air-raid

'Nice having the raid over early for once. I could do with a good night's sleep in me own bed.'

'Don't count your chickens. There's still a yellow alert on.'

'But the all-clear went!'

'That's the end of the red alert. The buggers are still hanging about somewhere. I think I'd better get me uniform on.' Mr McGill, foreman at the gasworks, knew such things.

'But your tea will be spoiled.'

'Put it back in the oven.'

Mrs McGill sniffed and picked up the *Daily Express* off the floor. Work-boots might never be cleaned, but ARP boots were always spotless and shining. Mr McGill, immaculate now, beret under shoulder strap, sat down again to eat.

Next moment, the lights went out. Then the cracks round the drawn black-out curtains lit up with successive streaks of light. Mr McGill's plate went crash on the floor.

'Oh those lovely sausages!' screamed his wife.

'Get down, hinny. Turn your face from the window. It's one of those sneak raiders.'

But it wasn't. Chas, lying face-down under the sofa heard the sound of many engines.

'Run for it!' They ran down the front passage and pulled open the front door. It was like day outside, there were so many parachute-flares falling. You could have seen a pin on the crazy-paving path to the shelter.

'The insurance policies!' screamed his mother, trying to turn back. His father stopped her bodily, and for a moment his parents wrestled like drunks in the front passage.

'Run, for God's sake,' panted his father.

The moment Chas set foot on the path outside, the bombs began to scream down. Chas thought his legs had stopped working for good; the black hole of the shelter door seemed to get further away instead of nearer. They said you never hear the bomb that hit you, but how could they know? Only the dead knew that, like the girl who had worked in the greengrocer's.

Chas saw the top half of her body, still obscenely weighing out potatoes . . .

Then he threw himself through the shelter door. He caught his knee on a corner of the bunk, and it was agony. Then his mother landed on top of him, knocking him flat, and he heard Dad's boots running, as he had never heard them before. Then a crack like thunder, and another and another and another and another. Great thunder-boots walking steadily towards them. The next would certainly crush them.

But the next never came; only the sound of bricks falling, like coalmen tipping coal into the cellar and glass breaking and breaking . . .

His father drew down the heavy tarpaulin over the shelter door, and his mother lit the little oil-lamp with her third trembling match. Then she lit the candle under a plant-pot that kept the shelter warm.

'Did you shut the front door, love?' she said to his father. 'I'm frightened someone'll nip in and steal those insurance-policies. And where's Mrs Spalding and Colin?'

Chug, chug, chug, chug.

'The buggers is coming again!' shouted Mr McGill. 'Where's the guns, where's the fighters?'

Above the chugging came a kind of rhythmic panting-screeching; and a kind of dragging-hopping, like a kangaroo in its death-throes. It was even more frightening than the chugging, and it came right up to the shelter-door. A body fell through. It was Mrs Spalding.

'Is she dead?' said Mrs McGill.

'No, but she's got her knickers round her ankles,' said Mr McGill.

'Aah had tey hop aal the way,' gasped Mrs Spalding. 'I was on the outside lav and I couldn't finish. The buggers blew the lav door off, and they've hit the Rex Cinema as well. Is there a spot of brandy?'

'Aah pulled the chain, Mam. It flushed all right.' It was Colin, with a self-satisfied smirk on his face.

'You'll get the Victoria Cross for that,' said Chas with a wild giggle.

'Shut-up, Charles. Have you got no feelings?' Mum turned to Mrs Spalding, who had crawled onto her bunk and was busy pulling up her knickers. 'I'm sorry, love. We got down the shelter so quick I left the brandy and the case behind. I'm worried about the insurance, too. Jack didn't shut the front door. Go back and get them, Jack!'

But the bombs had begun whining down again. Every time he heard one, Chas stared hard at the shelter wall. Mr McGill had painted it white, and set tiny bits of cork in the wet paint to absorb condensation. Chas would start to count inside his head. When the counting reached twenty, he would either be dead, or he would see little bits of cork fall off the shelter wall with the shock-wave, and know he had survived . . . till the next whistling started. It was a silly pointless game, with no real magic in it, but it stopped you wanting to scream . . .

His granda always said one only hit you if it had your name on it . . . he'd seen photographs of RAF blokes chalking names on their bombs . . . did the Germans do that too? . . . How would they know his name . . . did they have lists of everyone who lived in England . . .? Perhaps the Gestapo had . . . he must stop thinking like that, or he would scream . . . make a fool of himself like Mrs Spalding . . . play another game, quick.

TASKS

1 Look carefully at the children in the slit trench on p. 52. Imagine that they are silently praying. Write what you think their prayers would be. In groups, try to find a way of presenting these prayers dramatically.

2 In small groups, improvise a scene in which a number of young teachers try to find a way of getting their infants into the air-raid shelter without frightening them. What sort of language would they use? Invent a game which would make going to the shelter an adventure.

3 Draw a floor plan of an Anderson shelter. These shelters were buried at least three feet (91cm) deep with at least 18 inches (46cm) of earth piled on the roof for further protection. When completed, the whole unit measured at least 6ft x 6ft x 6ft

(2m x 2m x 2m). It had to hold up to eight people. What would you need to put in it? Where would everything go?

4 Using both the pictures on p. 52 and the extract from *The Machine Gunners* as a guide, devise a scene which is set in an air-raid shelter. Try to show how people deal with:
– the space;
– the cold;
– the blackout;
– the routine;
– the fear.

RATIONING

Rationing was first introduced in January 1940. As the war went on, more and more things were rationed. Here are some of them:

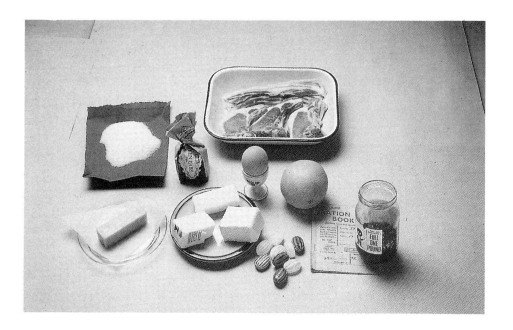

- Are there any things here which surprise you?
- Why do you think these things in particular had to be rationed?
- Which ones would you miss most?

1942-43 CLOTHING BOOK

This book may not be used until the holder's name, full postal address and National Registration (Identity Card) Number have been plainly written below IN INK.

NAME _____ S A BOADEN
(BLOCK LETTERS)

ADDRESS 'COOMBE DENE', HORSESHOE LANE
(BLOCK LETTERS)

(TOWN) WATFORD (COUNTY) HERTS

NATIONAL REGISTRATION (IDENTITY CARD) NUMBER

D F S H / 112 / 6

Read the instructions within carefully, and take great care not to lose this book

Page 1

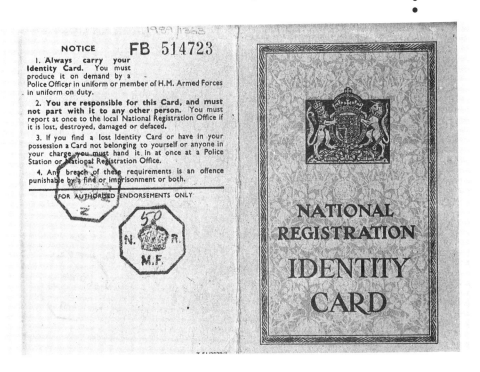

Everyone had a 'ration book', a clothing allowance and a National Identity Card. If you were caught not carrying your Identity Card, you could find yourself in serious trouble.

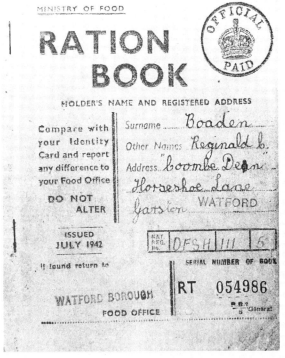

Eggless, Fatless Walnut Cake

4 cups flour   1 cup chopped walnuts
1 good cup milk 1 good pinch salt
1 cup sugar   4 teaspoons baking powder

Mix flour, sugar and chopped walnuts
together. Add salt and baking powder,
then the milk. It should be slightly wetter
than an ordinary cake mixture. Leave to
rise for 10 minutes. Bake in a greased cake
tin in a slow oven till risen and brown.

Black Pudding Toast

$^1/_2$lb black pudding   1 onion
seasoning   a little dripping
1 small cupful of oatmeal

Heat the dripping in a pan and add the
black pudding. Mash well and add
chopped onion and oatmeal. Stir for a few
minutes and cook gently till onion is
tender. Season. Serve on hot toast.

Sparrow Pie (not encouraged by the
Ministry)

12 sparrows & the occasional lark
bacon   mace
forcemeat   sage

Put a piece of bacon between each bird
and spread a leaf of mace, sage and a little
forcemeat on the top of the pie, under the
crust. Make a thickened gravy and add the
juice of a lemon and serve quickly.

Cheese Muffins

$1^1/_2$ cupfuls flour $^1/_2$ cupful grated cheese
$^1/_4$ teaspoon salt $^3/_4$ cupful milk
4 teaspoons baking powder 1 egg

Beat the egg lightly, add the salt and milk.
Sift the flour and baking powder together,
and then put in the grated cheese. Make

into a dough with the liquid, beat well and
roll out. Cut into rounds, brush with
beaten egg, and back for 10 minutes in a
sharp oven. Spread with butter eat hot.

Somerset Rook Pie with Figgy Paste

6 rooks
weak stock
pieces of fat bacon cut in chunks
pepper and salt to taste
For the paste
1lb flour
$^1/_2$lb fat
4oz currants
4oz raisins, stoned
pepper and salt to taste

Bake the rooks, which must have been
skinned, using only the legs and breast, as
all other parts are bitter. They should be
left soaking in salt and water overnight. In
the morning drain away the brine and put
the legs and breast in a good-sized pie-dish,
adding the fat bacon. Cover with the stock
and season well with pepper and salt.

For the paste, rub the fat well into the
flour, adding pepper and salt, then add the
currants and raisins. Mix well, and add
sufficient water to make a stiff paste. Roll
out to about $^3/_4$in thick, then place right
over the pie, letting it come well over the
sides. Cover the pie with a piece of
greaseproof paper, and then put the
pudding cloth on top. Tie well down and
see that the water has no chance of getting
in. There must be sufficient water in your
boiler to cover it. Do not put the pie in
until the water is boiling. The pie takes a
good 3 hours to cook, and is delicious
served with gooseberry jelly.

Lesley complains of how 'boring' everything is. Look at the list below and think what effect each of these would have on your own life:

— petrol rationed;

— clothes rationed;

— food rationed;

— blackout regulations (no light to be shown after dark);

— nearly all men aged over eighteen called into the army, airforce or navy;

— school leaving age, fourteen;

— women aged twenty to thirty ordered into military service or directed to work.

New regulations affected just about everything. New fashions, such as the pencil skirt were started, because pleats were banned as being wasteful.

A host of recipe suggestions appeared, attempting to make the most of limited ingredients. Some of these recipes are given on p.58. Why not try to make some of them!

Anyone caught breaking the regulations could be punished, as this extract from a local newspaper shows:

> ### BREAD WASTED
>
> Miss Mary Bridget O'Sullivan, Normandy Avenue, Barnet, Herts., was fined a total of ten pounds, with two guineas costs, at Barnet today for permitting bread to be wasted . . . It was stated that the servant was twice seen throwing bread to birds in the garden, and when Miss O'Sullivan was interviewed, she admitted that bread was put out every day.

Although many basic foods were rationed, chocolate and sweets were still available in limited quantities. Being full of energy-giving glucose, they were sometimes advertised as being a real contribution to the war effort:

TASKS

1 Imagine there was television during the War. In pairs, devise your own wartime cookery programme. Show viewers how to make delicious meals with the simplest ingredients.

2 Using the same television idea, devise a programme called, 'Tips for Teenagers', aimed at solving Lesley's boredom with the restrictions on clothes and entertainment.

3 Write the 'problem page' from a teen magazine of the period.

4 Hot-seat Miss O'Sullivan. Try to find out what she thinks of her punishment for feeding the birds. Will she be able to pay the fine? (Look back to the chart on p. 26 to see just how much ten pounds was worth).

5 Look at the advertisement for Fry's chocolate on P.60. Write, draw or act out an advertisement of your own, which shows how using the product will actually help win the War!

GOING HOME

The bombing raids became less frequent during 1941. More and more of the evacuees returned home.

In 1944, a new terror began when the Germans began to fire rockets called V–1s at London. Known as 'Doodlebugs', these new weapons flew too fast to be shot down, and they began yet another wave of evacuation. By the Spring of 1945, though, Hitler's army had been pushed back to Germany and the end of the War was in sight.

The evacuees gradually went home. Some of them stayed with their foster parents until the very end of the War.

Some evacuees even settled in the places that they had been evacuated to. If you live in a village that took evacuees, you may even know one. A headmaster told us:

The village I come from is in the Welsh Valleys. Because so many people there are called Jones or Williams, it's common there to give people another name which tells you who they are. So you get Jones the Baker or Jones the Butcher. Well, we had one lad who came down in 1940 and was billeted in the local pub. When the War ended, he stayed on. Do you know, he runs that pub now and even though he's over sixty, everybody still calls him Arthur the Evacuee.

The evacuation threw many people together. It also tore many families and friends apart. It's not suprising that most people who were evacuated, or put up evacuees, have very clear memories of what happened. For some, the experience has had a permanent affect on them and on the way they see things.

I was being interviewed on a television programme. The interviewer was concerned with my life as a newsman. Soon we began discussing my early life and I suddenly found myself relating for the first time the story of my days as an evacuee. As the interviewer began to dig deeper, I began to cry.

I never really became part of the family again.

I learned to appreciate so many things in life, and even today, I much prefer the country to the town.

I don't think I ever got over that unbelievable loneliness.

I wouldn't have missed my time as an evacuee for anything, for it added such a great deal to my character. It helped me to look after other people as much as myself, and put me on my own two feet.

As I write this letter, I'm still searching for the sister who went with me over forty years ago. I have not seen her since. I am now a mother and a grandmother and shudder when I think of my evacuation. I thank God none of my children will have to go through what I went through. How I survived to tell this tale, I shall never know.

What would it have been like for the 'last evacuee' mentioned in this extract from a village school log book?

1945

May 8 The War ending as from yesterday the School was closed for 2 days, "National Holiday."

10 Ascension Day. School re-opened for the morning. Registers were closed at 9 a.m.; school attended Service at Church as usual. School closed for the afternoon.

11 Mr. Reynish, H.M. Inspector called this afternoon.

18 Attendance for the week was 84·4%. School closed after to-day for Whitsun Holiday, 1 week

28 School re-opened this morning

June 1 Attendance 92·7%. Only 2 "Evacuees" remain in the School

8 Attendance was 88·8%, one Evacuee remains.

11 Requisition was received to-day.

15 The last official Evacuee child left the School at the end of last week. Number on roll is now 124, classified as Berkshire children.

25 School was closed for to-day: an additional "VE" holiday, owing to the closure of the Factory and businesses.

27 Afternoon school was advanced 20 minutes with

TASKS

1   Imagine that an old school in your area is being demolished. Amongst sackfuls of documents, you find the school log book for the War years. It has been badly damaged. 'Restore' the most interesting pages. What special incidents has the Head noted?

2   Try to find some orginal material of your own. Simply by asking people about their personal experiences, you will find a wealth of material which you can use in your own written and drama work.

But first, before rushing off with a tape recorder to interview people, it will be worth your time to prepare a number of questions to ask them. Questions which only call for a 'Yes' or 'No' answer won't give you much material on their own. You will need to ask more 'open-ended' questions, which will allow the people being interviewed the chance to give you detailed answers.

Compare the two lists of questions below. Which ones do you think will get the most detailed answers?

LIST ONE
'Were you in the army?'
'Did you get bombed?'
'Were you evacuated?'

'Did you enjoy the War?'
'Was it hard?'

LIST TWO
"How did you spend most of your time when you were in the army?'
'What was it like during the air-raids?'
'What do you remember about the evacuation?'
'Was the War all bad, or were there bits of it that you have good memories of?'
Practise your interview technique on each other first, to discover what general rules there are for interviewers. Can you add any more to this list?
– be polite;
– talk clearly, so that the questions are understood;
– prepare the questions in advance;
– listen carefully.

3   Set up a television show in which people who had an experience of evacuation are given the chance to talk about their memories. The show should be aimed at an audience that knows nothing about the evacuation. What factual information would you choose to give along with the personal memories?

MARTIN: A REFUGEE'S TALE

Although the government put a lot of pressure on parents to evacuate their children in 1939, it wasn't actually compulsory. What would it be like if you were told you **had** to leave your home?

What would it be like to be evacuated not to be kept safe, but because **you** were seen as a danger?

The story below is a true one. Reading it will show you another side to the evacuation.

Everybody thinks of the children at the stations in 1939, with their suitcases and labels: mums crying, trainloads of kids cheering. My experiences of evacuation were very different from all that.

I left my home in Germany in 1933. No-one would give me a job because I was a Jew. Even at that time, you'd see other families on the road pulling carts piled high with their belongings. The train I took was quite full of Hitler's brownshirts. They were the ones who cheered when we passed such families. I stayed quiet and pretended to read a book.

My father had arranged work for me in England. Getting into England was hard. At Dover they said, 'No, you can't come in. Who are you? Where's your permit?'. Eventually, it was sorted out. I got a permit but had to renew it every six months.

In 1936, things were getting worse and worse. I persuaded my parents to leave Germany also. When they arrived, their passports were stamped 'Refugees from Nazi Oppression'. I applied for a British passport in 1938, but war broke out before it was granted.

We were living in Newcastle-upon-Tyne. In 1940, all 'enemy aliens' were moved away from the coast. 'Enemy alien' – that was me! Can you believe it? So, Evacuation Number Two. We were given twenty-four hours to leave. Most of our possessions just had to be left behind. I sold my car for ten shillings.

You know, the foreman at my firm said to me that I got all I deserved. 'Wasn't it the Jews,' he said, 'who'd put Hitler up to this – to declare war on England?' I couldn't believe my ears.

A few weeks later, I had a knock on the door of my lodgings. It was six o'clock in the morning. I knew what it must mean. Plenty of my friends in Germany had had the same experience. A couple of detectives said, 'Would you please accompany us to the police station.' My father, my brother and myself were taken to a camp. It was muddy and overcrowded. Soon they started taking people out to the Isle of Man. They told us that some of us would be sent further away – 'for our own safety'. My brother and I went on a ship called the 'Dunera'.

When we got on board, our suitcases were taken off us. I saw them being sliced open with bayonets and the contents being thrown overboard. We thought we were going to Canada. We weren't – we were going to Australia. When we found out, a lot of the men went hysterical. We saw ourselves living forever behind barbed wire in the desert. You have to realise that many internees on the boat were children. They were only fourteen years of age, a lot of these children. They weren't accompanied by brothers or fathers. I don't know how they got there, but they were there all right. And there we were, in Australia for the duration of the War – and not a single person amongst us a Nazi parachutist!

I looked up 'evacuate' in the dictionary one time. Sure, it said 'to remove, as from a place of danger'. But it also said, 'to throw out, discharge'. I think I know both meanings.

QUESTIONS *to think and talk about*

- Martin says that he knows two meanings of the word 'evacuation'. The first meaning is to do with getting away from danger. Can you think of any other people who have been evacuated because they were in danger?

- Are people only ever evacuated in wartime? What other dangers might force people to move from their homes?

- Why did Martin leave Germany? Was he evacuated by others, or did he organise the 'evacuation' for himself?

- Can you think of any other groups of people who have left their homes for the same reasons as Martin left Germany in 1933?
- The second meaning of 'evacuate' is to do with 'getting rid of'. Who wanted to get rid of Martin? Why?
- Can you think of any other groups of people who are moved because they are not wanted?

Look at the two pictures below and the one overleaf. In what way are these people the same as the evacuees of the Second World War? Are there any differences?

Some people who have personal experiences of evacuation may never have told their stories. Perhaps the memories are too painful. Perhaps they have never been asked.

Martin's story is a true one. It has only recently been told publicly.

- How is Martin different from other evacuees?
- It is very difficult to find more information about the people taken to Australia on the SS Dunera. Why do you think this is?

Perhaps someone you know has a special story to tell. They may be people who remember the War and have memories of that evacuation.

There may also be people in your school or local area who have experienced a different sort of evacuation. What are their stories? Should they be told? Can they be told through drama?

JUST REMEMBER TWO THINGS: IT'S NOT FAIR AND DON'T BE LATE ....

by Terence Frisby

Just remember ... was first broadcast on BBC Radio in 1988. It's an autobiographical play, that is, it tells the story of what actually happened to the author.

Like many of the evacuees whose memories are printed in this book, Terence Frisby was evacuated from London to a country area. In his case it was Cornwall, though the people who put him up were in fact Welsh. In a way, Uncle Jack and Auntie Rose are themselves evacuees, having had to leave the Welsh valleys to look for work.

Staying in Cornwall for the whole of the war, Terence Frisby experienced many fearful and funny things. He was caught in the air raid that devastated Plymouth, saw a German bomber crash, had fights with the local children, fell out with the schoolteacher and saw a young evacuee friend killed by an army lorry. All this and discovering the facts of life with a girl called Elsie!

This extract comes from close to the start of *Just remember...* It introduces the characters and sets the atmosphere for the rest of the play.

CHARACTERS

NARRATOR	Terence Frisby himself spoke the Narrator's lines in the original broadcast; the whole play is, after all, his story.
TERRY	A bright seven year old.
JACK	His older brother, aged eleven.
UNCLE JACK AUNTIE ROSE }	An oldish Welsh couple who put Terry and Jack up in their home in Cornwall.
MUM	
DRIVER	

THE PLAY

NARRATOR   I was the luckiest of children: I had two childhoods. My earliest memories are of pre-war, antiseptic Welling, just in Kent but really suburban London. . . Then came the war and my other childhood. A few days after the last British soldiers left Dunkirk, when my brother, Jack was eleven and I was seven, we became evacuees – vaccies – and were carried off to another world.

Fade in bedroom. Packing. The boys are excited. Mum is nearly cracking.

TERRY.   Are you gonna stay here and fight the Germans, Mum?

MUM.   Come here, Terry, while I tie this label on you.

TERRY.   Aaagh, it's got my name and address on it.

MUM.   That's right.

TERRY.   I know who I am.

MUM.   Of course you do. That's there in case – (*She stops and the bright exterior nearly cracks.*) – in case you get lost.

TERRY.   I can *tell* 'em who I am.

JACK (*taunting*).   's in case the Germans gag you and you can't speak.

TERRY (*intrigued*).   Honest?

MUM.   Be quiet, Jack. Come here.

JACK.   Ah, no. I'm not having one too, am I?

MUM.   Yes.

JACK.   I'm four years older'n him.

MUM.   Stand still.

TERRY.   Westmoreland Secondary school. Form Two C. Huh-hah. You're a C. Rotten Cs. I'm an A.

JACK.   Big head.

MUM (*sharply*).   Stop that. (*The boys are silent, surprised.*) Listen, you two. Cs and As don't matter. He's your brother, Terry. You do as he says. He's older than you.

TERRY (*sulkily*).   I'm cleverest.

MUM.   I'm clever*er*, smart Alec, and you're not. Now you do as Jack says and you stay with him. No rows. Got it?

TERRY .   All right.

MUM (*mum is fighting the tears of anxiety*).   And you look after him, Jack. D'you hear me?

JACK.   'kay, Mum.

MUM.   You're his big brother. Don't you stand any nonsense from him and don't you *dare* leave him. You stay together, d'you hear?

JACK.   Can I bash him?

TERRY (*starts to protest*).   No, I'm not going to let him –

MUM. *No.* (*She pauses.*) Well – if he's naughty – I – no. Oh, come on, you two, help me.

TERRY.   I can look after myself, Mum.

MUM.   All right, all right. You look after each other. How's that? D'you hear? You both look after each other.

JACK. I'm 11. I don't need him –
MUM. *D'YOU HEAR ?*

> *Pause. Then mumbles of agreement.*

> That's right. That's good boys.
TERRY. You're the big head.
JACK. You wait till we get on that train.
MUM. Now, listen, both of you. Look here. See this? It's a postcard. It's a secret
code. Read it, Jack.
JACK (*haltingly*). Dear Mum and Dad, arrived safe and well. Ever-y-thing fine.
Love, Jack and Terry.
MUM. When you get there –
TERRY. Where?
MUM. Where you're going.
JACK (*whispers*) She doesn't know where.
MUM (*overlapping*). Find out the address. You can do that, Jack, can't you?
(*Pause.*) Well, can you?
JACK. Well . . .
MUM. Just ask someone.
JACK. Oh, yeah.
MUM. That's right. Both of you. Ask. Stay together and put the address where they
send you in that space there. Have you got that?
JACK. Is that all? Is that the code?
MUM. No. Now this is it. Our secret. You know how to write kisses?
TERRY. Ergh.
JACK. With a cross.
MUM. That's right. You put one kiss if it's nasty and I'll come straight there and
bring you back. At once. D'you see? You put two kisses if its all right and
three kisses if it's nice. (*Her voice cracks.*) Then I'll know.
NARRATOR. Mum walked us under a canopy of barrage balloons to the 89 bus-stop
by the We Anchor In Hope. They were digging up the golf course on Shooters
Hill to put anti-aircraft guns there and in Oxleas Wood opposite. At Welling
station several hundred yelling, rampant children were puffed away to adventure

*Fade in background. Many children yelling and cheering exuberantly. Steam
engine starting up and drawing away.*

NARRATOR. while Mum stood smiling and waving in a crowd of smiling waving
mums. She told us later she went home and sobbed . . . It seemed all South London
was out there waving. Jack said he saw Dad in one place, I in another. Dad said he
saw both of us but all any bystander could see

> *Faint children yelling and cheering from excitement.*

of that train was that it sprouted yelling juvenile heads and waving arms . . . We
eventually pulled up at a station in a cutting.

> *Locomotive stationary, releasing steam.*

Liskeard, said the boards. We couldn't even pronounce it. Cornwall, we were told.
A wall of corn. It sounded all right . . .

Fade in: murmur of Cornish voices. Interior school room.

NARRATOR. A crowd was waiting for us and, as we were taken into the main classroom, these people, strange in voice and manner, pushed in after us curiously, while we stared at them.

Crowd and children moving.

VOICES (*soft, very Cornish*). Hallo, my lover.

Here, come on, move on, next.

There y'are my 'andsome.

Over there, you go.

Outside, the toilet . . .

VOICES. I'll ave 'ee.

Er can come wi' I.

This one yere'll do me.

Come on, you. Want to come with me?

A child starts crying . . .

FEMALE VOICE (*Cornish accent*). What about you? You coming wi' me?

TERRY. I'm with my brother.

FEMALE VOICE (*Cornish accent*). Two of you, eh?

TERRY. Yes. Him.

JACK. Yes. We're staying together.

FEMALE VOICE (*Cornish accent*). Hm. Two boys is a bit much for us. (*Moving away.*) What about you, my 'andsome. Have you got a brother or sister?

GIRL'S VOICE (*off*). No.

Feet. Voices.

Auntie Rose is about 50, has a strong South-Wales accent.

AUNTIE ROSE. Yere. I'll have this one yere.

TERRY. Ow, that's my hair.

AUNTIE ROSE. Yes, I know, boy. Could do with a cut, too.

TERRY. You've got to have my brother, too.

AUNTIE ROSE. What?

TERRY. Mum said we got to stay together. She said so.

AUNTIE ROSE. Did she, now? Are you his brother?

JACK. Yes, we're staying together.

AUNTIE ROSE. Are you now?

JACK. Yes. Together.

TERRY. Both of us.

AUNTIE ROSE. That's right, then. If your Mam said. How old you boys?

JACK Eleven.

TERRY. I'm seven.

AUNTIE ROSE. I like boys. Less trouble than girls. Girls, Oh, Dieu. (*She pronounces it dew.*) Nimby-pimby. All tears and temper . . .

(*Calls.*) Here y'are, Jack. We got two. Brothers. They got to stay together.

UNCLE JACK. Oh, Dieu, girl. Can we fit 'em in?

AUNTIE ROSE. Easy. We'll think of something. Come on boys, quick, before he changes his mind.

Cut to car moving. Interior.

NARRATOR. We headed out into more open country again, past a farm with a huddle of outbuildings which grimly showed their backs to the south-westerlies. Our driver broke the uncertain silence.

DRIVER (*broad east-Cornish accent*). They be everywhere, you know; they vaccies.

UNCLE JACK. Ay. All over.

DRIVER. St Neot, Menheniot; down to Duloe, up over Callington. The whole county's full of 'em. Didn't know they had so many kids in Lunnon. We got more 'n fifty to Dobwalls alone. Two down yere to Crago's farm. Three over to Polmeer's. Two boys at Miss Kitto's, the district nurse. Won't know if we'm coming 'r going, will us?

UNCLE JACK. Yere that, boys? Yere what the driver says?

Silence.

Wha's up? Cat got your tongues?

TERRY. Is he talking English?

The men laugh.

DRIVER. No, tint English. Tis Cornish. Don't you fret, my handsome, we'll have you talking Cornish yet.

UNCLE JACK. I'll watch it. Not living with a Welshman they won't. I'll tan it out of 'em.

The men laugh

JACK. Is your name really Jack?

UNCLE JACK. 'Course it is. What d'you think? We're telling fibs?

JACK. My name's Jack, too.

UNCLE JACK. Well, there is funny.

AUNTIE ROSE. We'll have to make sure we don't muddle you up, then.

UNCLE JACK. D'you think you can manage to tell the difference?

All laugh.

What you laughing at. We look just the same, don't we?

TERRY. He's younger'n you.

UNCLE JACK. No. Not much.

JACK. I've got hair.

AUNTIE ROSE *and* DRIVER *laugh.*

DRIVER. 'A's i'. You tell 'im.

UNCLE JACK. Oh, cheeky, are we?

DRIVER. Reckon he's got your mark, Jack Phillips.

TERRY (*over-encouraged by the laughter*). And you're redder and fatter. And you talk funny.

DRIVER. Hoo-hoo. Tha's 'cos he's Welsh. They'm heathens. Can't speak English not more'n we can.

The DRIVER *and* UNCLE JACK *laugh.*

JACK. Please, I'm sorry. He didn't mean anything.

AUNTIE ROSE. 'as all right, boy. He's only saying what he sees and hears.

UNCLE JACK. There's our house, see? Last one on the end of the row there.

NARRATOR. We stared at a row of Victorian cottages in the distance; more slate and

granite. They looked tiny and grim. Seven of them, as it turned out. How
could seven families live in so little space?

... Our address was 7 Railway Cottages. Our foster parents were Jack and
Rose Phillips, Auntie Rose and Uncle Jack to everybody in Doublebois. He
was a South Wales miner turned platelayer on the Great Western Railway.
Their own son and daughter were grown up; she, married and he in uniform in
the desert. That night, in the secrecy of the tiny back bedroom Jack and I
stared at Mum's postcard and considered our code.

*Fade in: interior boys' bedroom. They are either whispering or keeping their voices
very quiet.*

JACK. How many kisses shall we put?

TERRY. I vote three.

JACK. Hm. I'm not sure.

Door opening.

AUNTIE ROSE. Come on yere, you two. What's all this? Up-a-dando, into bed.

Drawer opening.

What are you hiding there?

JACK. Nothing.

Drawer close.

AUNTIE ROSE. Come on, then. Who's going at which end?

TERRY. Can I go this end, Mrs Phillips? In the corner?

AUNTIE ROSE. All right with you, young Jack?

JACK. Well.

He stops, embarrassed.

AUNTIE ROSE. Well what?

JACK. Will there be enough air for him in the corner? (*He pauses awkwardly.*)
 He's ever so small – smaller than he looks.

TERRY. I'm not.

AUNTIE ROSE (*most gently*). I think there will, boy. We'll open the window, is it?

JACK. Thank you, but –

TERRY. Oh, no.

JACK. I must.

AUNTIE ROSE. Must what, boy?

JACK. He gets asthma.

TERRY. I don't. Not much.

AUNTIE ROSE. All right, all right. I won't tell anyone. . . We'll open the window,
 there'll be lots of air and he'll be able to breathe there in the corner, you take
 my word . . . Did your Mam tell you to see about the air?

JACK. No, I thought it myself.

AUNTIE ROSE. Did you now? You're a fine boy. Now into bed, go on. No. Wait a
 minute. Do you say your prayers at night?

Pause.

Well, do you?

JACK (*surprised*). No.

AUNTIE ROSE. All right, then. In you get. My Jack's a heathen, too, but I'll say a prayer for both of you. Look, boys, if you want to go outside during the night, you got this yere. D'you see? Under the bed.

Chamber pot being set down on lino.

JACK. Why should we go outside?

AUNTIE ROSE. Why? Well, if you want to go down the garden, of course. To the privy.

JACK. Oh, yes. Outside. Sorry, Mrs Phillips.

AUNTIE ROSE. Auntie Rose, I said you call me. Right? (*Pause.*) Well?

JACK. But you're not our Auntie. Our Auntie's in Peckham.

AUNTIE ROSE. No, no I'm not. You're right. You call me Auntie Rose when you want to, is it? . . . Now I'm going to put out the candle if you're ready.

JACK. Could you leave it, please?

AUNTIE ROSE. Don't you like the dark?

JACK. No, it's not that. We got to –

AUNTIE ROSE. It's bedtime now.

JACK. We got to send a card to Mum and Dad.

AUNTIE ROSE. This one?

Drawer being opened.

JACK. Yes.

Drawer being closed.

AUNTIE ROSE. Is that your writing? It's very grown-up.

JACK. No, it's Mum's.

AUNTIE ROSE (*surprised*). She's already written the card.

TERRY. We got to put your address on it.

AUNTIE ROSE. Well, you've done it, haven't you. (*Chuckles.*) Yes, that's more like your writing. That's not how you spell Liskeard. I'll do you another card in the morning. A nice new one with a picture, how's that?

JACK (*panics*). No, no. We got to put something else on.

AUNTIE ROSE. Wha's that?

Pause.

Well?

JACK. Er – kisses.

AUNTIE ROSE (*little gentle laugh*). Well, all right, then. We can do that, too, in the morning.

JACK. *We* want to do it.

TERRY. By ourselves . . .

AUNTIE ROSE. All right, then. I'll leave the candle a bit and then come back again, is it, and watch you put out the candle the right way. We don't want a fire, do we? Your Mam wouldn't like that.

Door closing.

JACK (*whispers*). How many kisses?

TERRY. I vote three.

JACK. Perhaps we should take one off 'cos we've only got one bed.

TERRY. It's triffic here. 'S like being on holiday only there's no sea.

JACK. What about no electricity?

TERRY. I don't care.

JACK. And no indoor lav.

TERRY I don't care.

JACK. How many shall we put, then?

NARRATOR. We ringed the card with kisses and posted it next morning. It made no difference, Mum still turned up unannounced within the week. Just to make sure.

ACTING THE PLAY

1 When Mum is helping the boys to pack, why does she pause in the middle of her line:

That's the case — (She stops and the bright exterior nearly cracks) – in case you get lost.

What might she be thinking?

In pairs, try saying this line in a way that shows:

- what she's really thinking **and**
- that she's trying hard not to let the boys know she's thinking it

2 Jack taunts his brother Terry when he says ''s in case the Germans gag you and you can't speak.'

- Does Terry believe him?
- Does Jack always tease Terry?
- How well do you think the brothers get on with each other?

In pairs, pick out three incidents or lines from the extract which you think show different aspects of their relationship. Make a still picture of each one.

Compare your choices with another pair's.

3 *Just remember. . .* needs actors to speak in different accents:

LONDON   CORNISH   WELSH

How well can you manage any of these parts? In threes, try out some of the lines spoken in the taxi and see if you can capture a different accent for each.

4 Why do you think the boys choose to 'ring the card with kisses'?

What is it about Jack and Rose that causes the boys to react so warmly to them?

As a group, hot-seat two volunteers as Jack and Rose. Try to find out more about them which seems to fit with what is already in this extract.

PRODUCING THE PLAY

1   As he was writing a radio play, Terence Frisby had to rely on a lot of sound effects to give his audience a clear mental picture of what was going on in his memory.
- Make a note of all the different sound effects he uses in this extract. How long should each one last? Should they stop suddenly or fade out?
- Make up a sound cue sheet like the one below which gives details on how the sound effects should be added. Don't add sound that you think the actors would make on their own e.g. (mumbles of agreement).

2   BBC Sound Effects records are available through most libraries. Use your cue sheet to find the records you would need and, if possible, experiment with making up a soundtrack for this extract.

How else might you make the sounds?
Experiment both with objects and your own voices.

3   As a whole group, set up the scene in the schoolroom. Various lines are suggested for background VOICES. How would you bring these in to a recording of the play? Are they enough?
- Try reading exactly as they are printed.
- Try improvising your own suitable lines. Which sounds most realistic?

Is it possible to fade improvised lines up and down so that the main characters can be clearly heard? Try to devise a signal which will tell the VOICES when they should build the atmosphere and when they should simply be in the background.

4   How could you organise your drama space into a suitable area in which to act out this extract?

You will need to think where to put four scenes:

THE BEDROOM   THE SCHOOLROOM
THE TAXI   THE COTTAGE BEDROOM

How could you suggest each scene simply by using a few objects? What objects would you use?

Draw a plan of your drama space. Find a way of showing where each scene should take place, where the audience should be and how the audience will know where the scene is.

SOUND CUES: JUST REMEMBER . . .			
Cue No	Description	Duration	Instruction
1	Packing suitcase	60 secs	5 secs for atmosphere then as background to end scene.
2	Children yelling/ steam engine	10 secs	Fade in on 'adventure'. Lines to carry on over sound. Fade out.

IDEAS FOR DRAMA

1   In small groups, invent two contrasting scenes which you think would fit into this play.

One should show an incident that Terence Frisby would remember as being funny (though it may not have felt that way at the time). The other should show something that he will always feel either sad or angry about. You might get some ideas for your scenes by looking at the introduction to the extract on p. 69.

2   Terry stayed with Uncle Jack and Auntie Rose for the whole of the war, then went back to London. Improvise a suitable last scene for the play. You may or may not decide to actually show the scene in which Terry says goodbye to Uncle Jack and Auntie Rose. Consider the advantages and disadvantages of such a scene. Are there other alternatives?

IDEAS FOR WRITING

1   Imagine that Terry and Jack send a number of postcards home during their stay in Cornwall. Make up the five which, for one reason or another, you think their mum would want to keep.

2   How do you write accents down accurately?

Imagine someone with a particularly strong accent from another area or country has stopped you to ask for directions. Write the dialogue down in a way that you think captures your accent and theirs.

3   Imagine you are either Terry or his brother, Jack. The teacher in the village school has asked you to write about one of the following
*   your life back home near London;
*   the day you were evacuated;
*   your new life in the countryside.